Breathe Deep,
LITTLE SHEEP

Andrews McMeel Publishing
a division of Andrews McMeel Universal
1130 Walnut Street, Kansas City, Missouri 64106
www.andrewsmcmeel.com

20 21 22 23 24 HUH 10 9 8 7 6 5 4 3 2 1

ISBN: 978-1-5248-6535-1

Library of Congress Control Number: 2020941108

Editor: Allison Adler
Designer: Katie Jennings Campbell
Production Editor: Jasmine Lim
Production Manager: Chuck Harper

ATTENTION: SCHOOLS AND BUSINESSES
Andrews McMeel books are available at quantity discounts with bulk purchase
for educational, business, or sales promotional use. For information, please e-mail the
Andrews McMeel Publishing Special Sales Department: specialsales@amuniversal.com.

Made by: Hung Hing Printing (China) Co., Ltd
Address and place of production:
Hung Hing Industrial Park, Fu Yong Town,
Shenzhen, 518103 China
1st Printing—11/23/20

Breathe Deep, LITTLE SHEEP

A Calm-Down Book for Kids

JESSICA LEE illustrated by LUCIA WILKINSON

Andrews McMeel
PUBLISHING®

Don't be nervous, little pup,
the storm will soon be over.

Close your eyes and picture this:
a field of flowers and clover.

Shake a feather, little penguin.
Don't just stand in place.

Moving shakes the worries loose,
so come, let's have a race!

It's tempting when you're anxious
to curl up tight and hide.

But open up and use your words.
Say how you feel inside!

If you feel your heart start pounding
and you're breathing way too fast,

collect yourself and say these words:
exhale, release, relax.

When a problem feels enormous
and you don't know what to do,

just break it into little steps:
one hop, two hops, go you!

Slow down, little squirrel.
You just need a quiet spot . . .

to feel the breeze and hear the birds
and rest your busy thoughts.

Breathe deep, little sheep.
There's no need for alarm.

Inhale, exhale, then repeat.
You're learning to stay calm.

There are lots of simple strategies kids can use when anxiety strikes. The more strategies kids learn, the more confident they'll feel. Try this mindful breathing exercise along with your child. Teach them that this is one of many tools they can use to handle life's ups and downs.

STEP 1: Ask your child to breathe in gently through their nose and out through their mouth. Explain to them that paying attention to their breath can help them calm down. It can also give them clues as to how they're feeling.

STEP 2: Hand them a pinwheel to hold up to their face and encourage them to make it spin slowly as they exhale deeply and gradually. If they enjoy this, they can also try a bubble wand, a dandelion, or a tissue to "see" what mindful, gentle breathing looks like.

STEP 3: Explain to your child that taking deep, slow breaths can help them feel more relaxed at school, at home, in the car, and anywhere they go.